Dedicated
to all of the
parents
raising little
ones during these
difficult times.

we got this.

STORY & DRAWINGS BY
amy pye

Bruce the silly goose

Bruce was a silly goose.

He would not wear a mask.

...and stomped his feet whenever his friends would ask.

He wouldn't even wash his hands, a task that seems quite small.

He just
refused
and shook
his head.

He would not
wash
at all.

But Bruce, said his friends, this isn't just about you!

We need to stop germs from spreading around.

Let's keep the whole world safe and sound!

Bruce
listened
to the advice
that his friends
shared

and he knew it
meant
that they
really
cared!

Bruce did **not** want his friends to get ill,

So he
said
OK!
For you
guys
I will.

Lightning Source UK Ltd.
Milton Keynes UK
UKHW050728221220
375685UK00002B/72